Helena Clare Pittman ONCE
WHEN I WAS SCARED

illustrated by Ted Rand

E. P. DUTTON
NEW YORK

When Grandfather was a boy and lived upstate in the mountains, his mother sent him to get hot coals from the neighbors next door. Next door was across two hills and through a dark wood.

The stove had gone out, and dank air now seeped through the walls of the cabin. After a week of steady autumn drizzle, the woodpile was too damp to kindle coal.

Grandfather's mother took the tin box with the wooden handle down from the shelf.

"Don't go wandering, Daniel," she said as she looked uneasily through the curtains at the sky. "It feels like a storm is coming."

Daniel pushed his feet into his boots and put on his coat.

Then he picked up the box,
stepped outside, and headed
toward the woods.

A few fiery autumn leaves still
clung to the trees, the only bright
color in the foggy valley. They
shivered in the wind, which stung
Daniel's cheeks.

"Hurry back!" his mother
called. "It will be dark soon."

But her voice sounded far away. Daniel was already sliding, half falling through the wet leaves, down the far side of the first hill.

The wind blew smoky-looking clouds across the sky and whistled through the holes in the sides of the coal box. Daniel stumbled over slippery rocks and roots as he tried to run. Tangles of branches caught his woolen leggings, slowing him.

But suddenly he broke free.
Now he moved easily over the
roots, springing gracefully off
rocks with his strong back legs.
His sharp claws dug into the
leaves. Behind him a silvery
tail bounced on the wind, its
white tip a bright flicker in
the shadows.

Then he was knocking at the Nickersons' door, his heart pounding.

"Come in, Daniel," Mrs. Nickerson said with a friendly smile. "Catch your breath and warm yourself."

"Mama is waiting," he panted. "May I have some coals? Our fire went out."

Mrs. Nickerson filled his tin box with coals from the stove and snapped the lid shut. The box felt warm in his hands as she rewrapped his muffler snugly under his chin.

"Good night, Daniel," she called as he left the clearing.

In the dark wood, Daniel started to run. Soon he was covered with sweat underneath his warm clothes. An owl hooted in a tree above him. As he looked up, something caught his foot and he fell. He struggled to free himself but it wrapped more tightly around his legs. In the shadows it looked like a snake.

Gripping the box, he twisted over like a cat. A big cat. A bobcat.

In a second he bounded away, free. His balance was sure. He was long and lithe. His paws made no sound as he leaped again and again over the fallwood and underbrush.

He could see the hill behind his house, when suddenly he heard a crash of branches. Ahead was a huge black shape. It looked like a bear, crouching. The fur on its neck stood straight up. He heard it snarl. A bear stood between him and home.

In the place of his cat's paws were his leather boots and mittened hands. Shaking, he dropped the tin box. The lid fell open and coals scattered, hissing on the wet ground.

The bear turned and rose on
its back legs. Daniel jumped
back. He felt himself rise off
the ground. His feet became
talons, his arms huge dark
wings that lifted him up above
the bear. He shouted at the
top of his voice to frighten it.
The sound that came from
his throat was the shriek of
an eagle.

The bear lumbered off into the woods. Moonlight flickered through churning clouds as the great bird landed in the leaves.

Daniel took a long, deep breath, then looked at himself. His wings were gone. He was wearing his coat, which was matted with dirt, and his muffler was still wound around his neck.

Then he knelt and put the glowing coals back into the tin box. He brushed off his clothes, picked up the box, and climbed the hill.

Rain was just beginning to fall as he reached home.

"How quickly you went and came, Daniel," said his mother. She held him close. Her warmth felt good against his cheek. "Hardly fifteen minutes passed since you left!" She took the coals and laid a bed in the stove for the kindling. Flames soon danced through the crackling twigs.

"Did it really happen, Grandfather?" I asked.

"I found these in my coat the next day," answered my grandfather. He held out two stiff pinion feathers. By their markings they could only have come from an eagle.

He gave them to me, once when I was scared. I put those feathers in my drawer, where I still keep them. Sometimes, when I feel afraid, I take them out. I hold them in my fingers and remember the look in my grandfather's eyes when he gave them to me.

To Albert V. Jessen,
who gave me a feather to keep
H.C.P.

To my son, Martin,
the boy in the forest
T.R.

Text copyright © 1988 by Helena Clare Pittman
Illustrations copyright © 1988 by Ted Rand
Published in the United States by
E. P. Dutton, a division of
Penguin Books USA Inc.
Published simultaneously in Canada by
Fitzhenry & Whiteside Limited, Toronto
Designer: Barbara Powderly
Printed in Hong Kong by South China Printing Co.
First Edition   W   10 9 8 7 6 5 4 3 2

Library of Congress Cataloging-in-Publication Data
Pittman, Helena Clare.
    Once when I was scared / by Helena Pittman; illustrated
by Ted Rand.—1st ed.
        p.   cm.
    Summary: Grandfather tells how, when he was a child,
he coped with fear during a journey alone through a dark
wood to get hot coals to heat the family cabin.
    ISBN 0-525-44407-6
    [1. Fear—Fiction.]   I. Rand, Ted, ill.   II. Title.
PZ7.P689On   1988   88-3598
[E]—dc19   CIP
                                             AC